Rocky
The Christmas Owl

Written and Illustrated by

Bobbie Gilbert Kogok

DEDICATION

Dedicated to all my family, friends, and readers,
may you always find the small miracles that are present in our lives every day!

Many thanks to all the kind folks who helped Rocky on her journey,
especially the experts at The Ravensbeard Wildlife Center.

Christmas is always

a time of good cheer;

Although, two thousand

twenty had been a rough year!

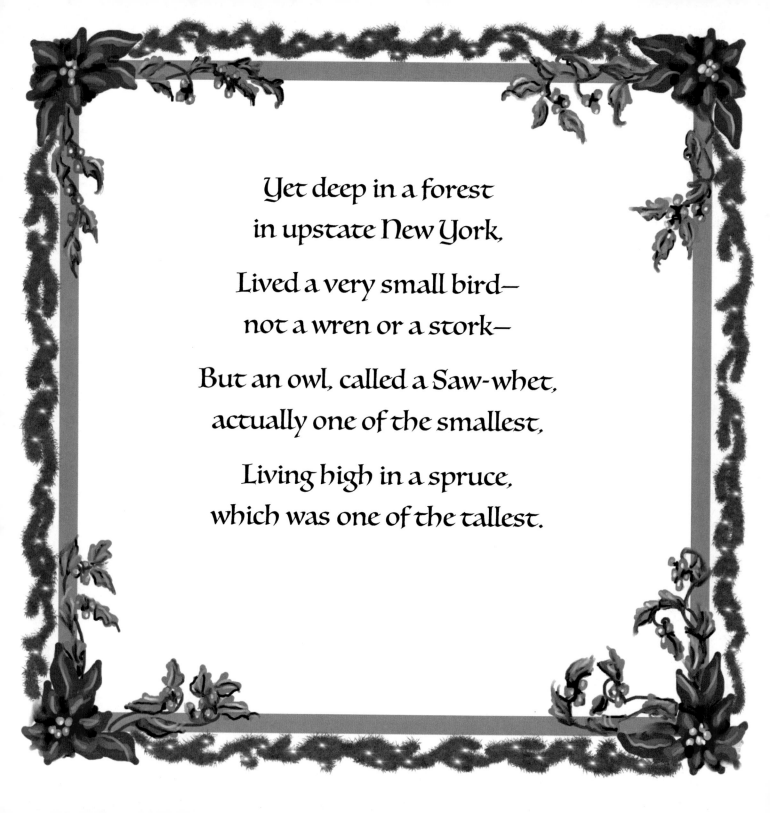

Yet deep in a forest
in upstate New York,

Lived a very small bird—
not a wren or a stork—

But an owl, called a Saw-whet,
actually one of the smallest,

Living high in a spruce,
which was one of the tallest.

Oneonta, NY
City of the Hills
Pop. 13,901

Oneonta, NY
City of the Hills
Pop. 13,901

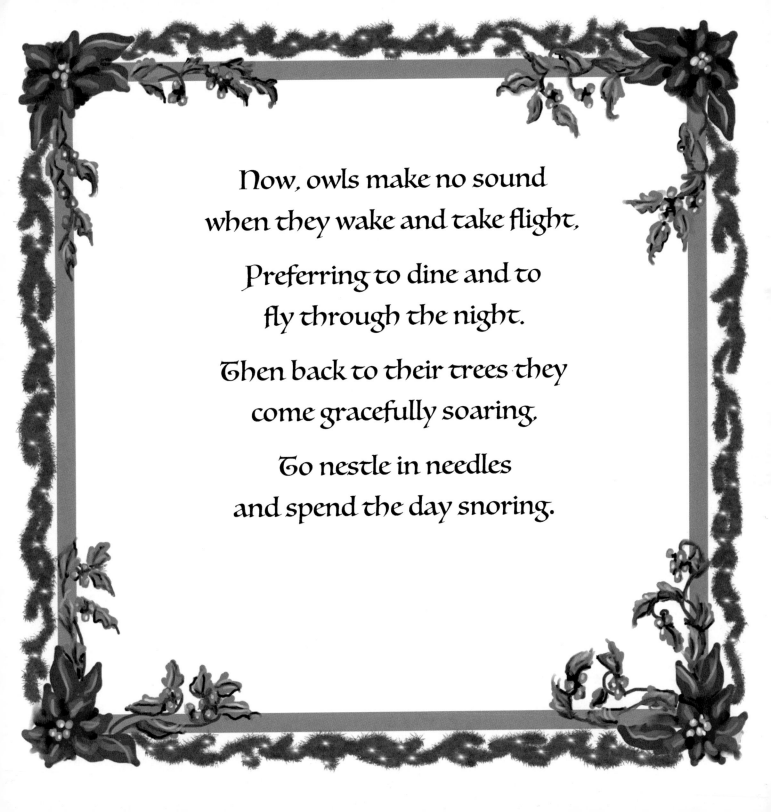

Now, owls make no sound
when they wake and take flight,

Preferring to dine and to
fly through the night.

Then back to their trees they
come gracefully soaring,

To nestle in needles
and spend the day snoring.

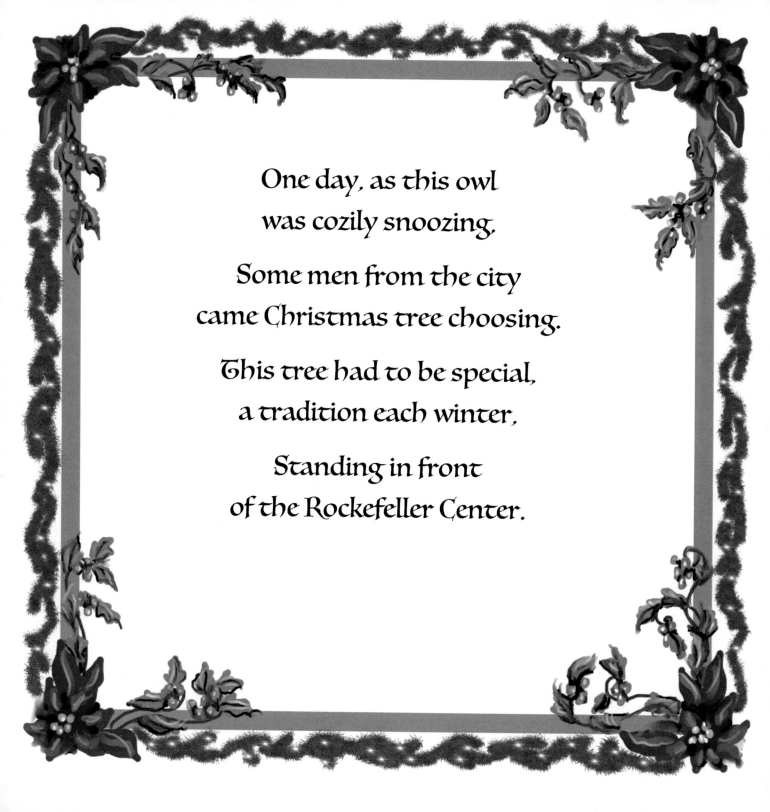

One day, as this owl
was cozily snoozing,

Some men from the city
came Christmas tree choosing.

This tree had to be special,
a tradition each winter,

Standing in front
of the Rockefeller Center.

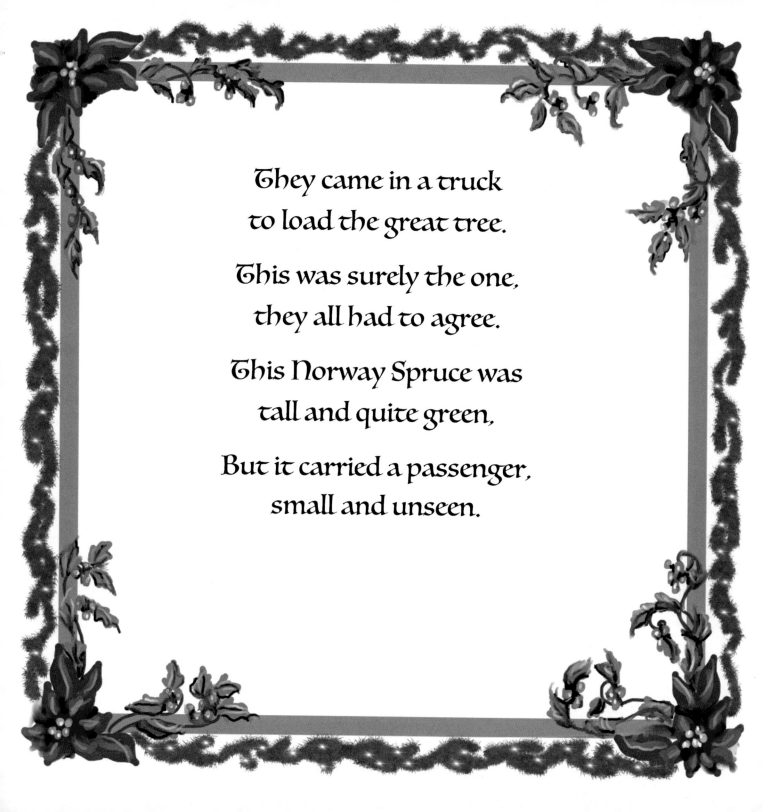

They came in a truck
to load the great tree.

This was surely the one,
they all had to agree.

This Norway Spruce was
tall and quite green,

But it carried a passenger,
small and unseen.

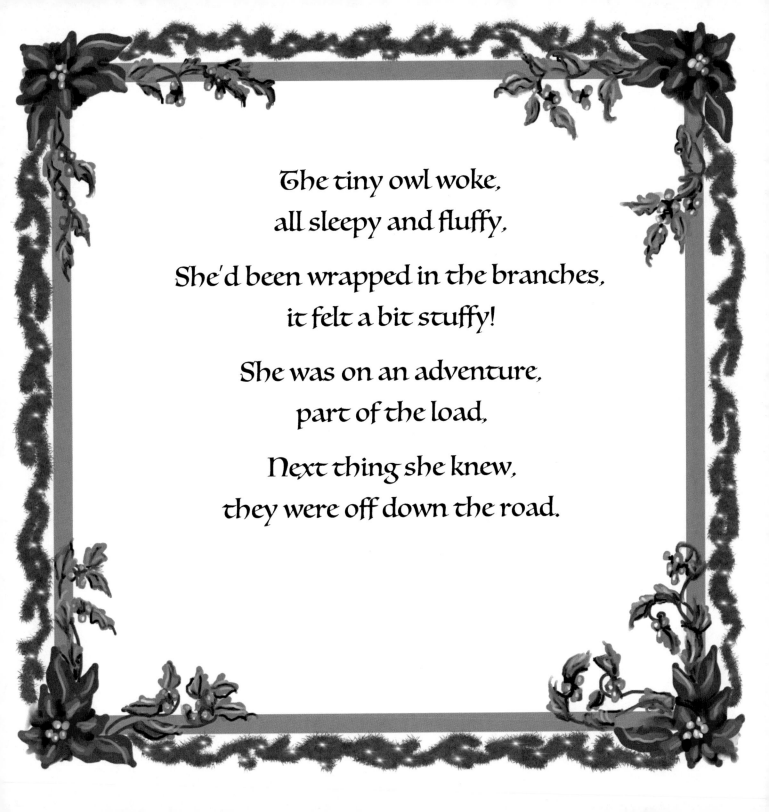

The tiny owl woke,
all sleepy and fluffy,

She'd been wrapped in the branches,
it felt a bit stuffy!

She was on an adventure,
part of the load,

Next thing she knew,
they were off down the road.

They traveled all-day
and then through the night.

She wanted to stretch,
to eat, and take flight!

Again through a day
and night the truck rumbled.

She needed a drink
and her poor tummy grumbled.

Finally, the truck took a turn,
it was slowing,

Time to unload the tree
it was towing.

Off came the cords,
the twine and the rope,

Loosening the branches,
which gave the owl hope.

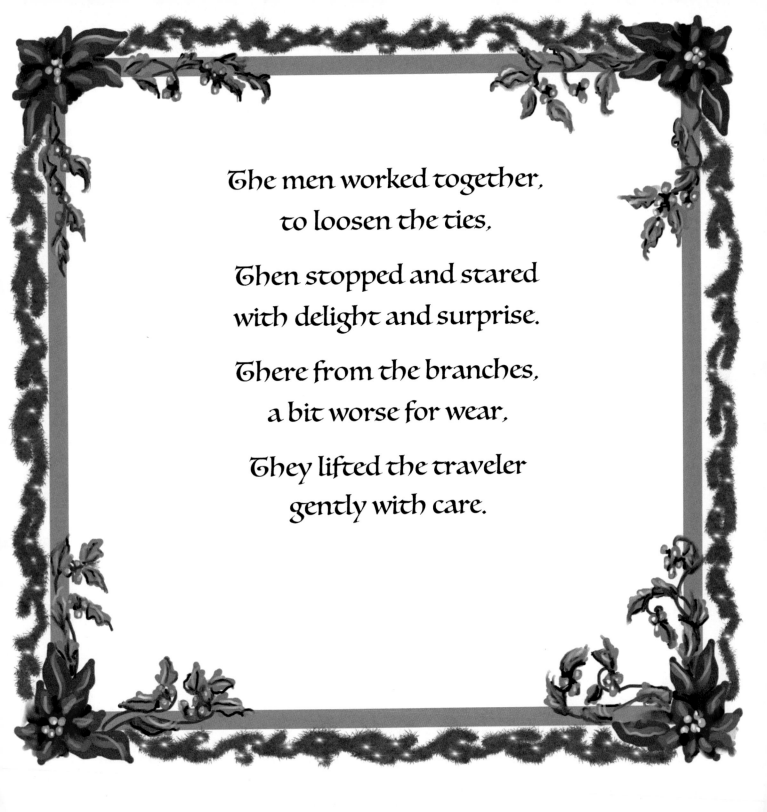

The men worked together,
to loosen the ties,

Then stopped and stared
with delight and surprise.

There from the branches,
a bit worse for wear,

They lifted the traveler
gently with care.

She was so tiny,
so fluffy and sweet,

And so very hungry—
she needed to eat.

She'd made the long trip
and fared rather well.

After two days of pampering,
she felt pretty swell.

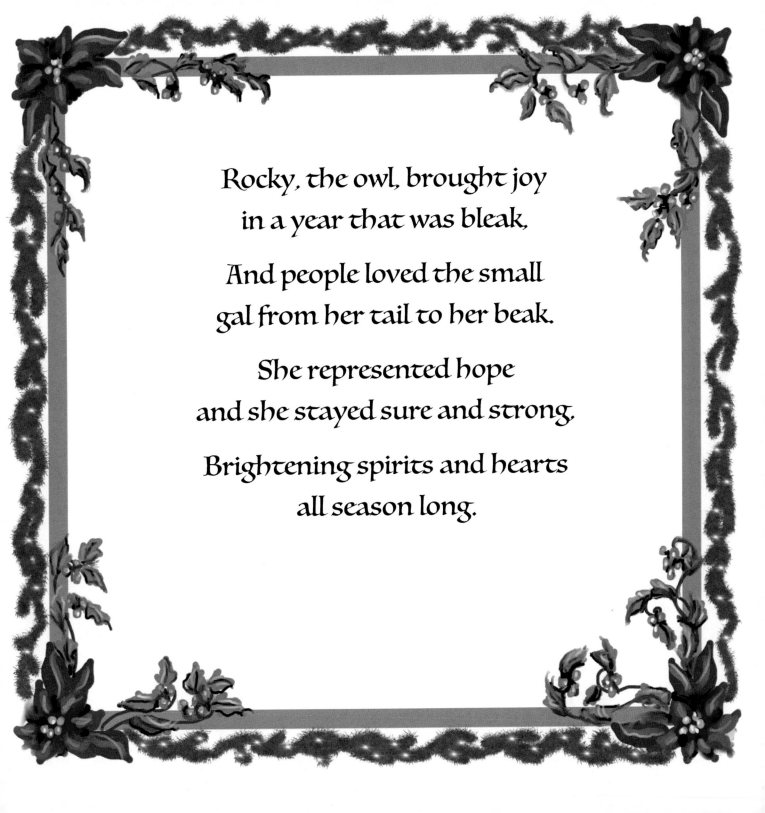

Rocky, the owl, brought joy
in a year that was bleak,

And people loved the small
gal from her tail to her beak.

She represented hope
and she stayed sure and strong,

Brightening spirits and hearts
all season long.

Although not residing
in Central Park now,

Rocky still visits the
City's green boughs.

And if you are watching
this holiday night,

You might see her taking
her Christmas Eve flight.

Hope you have enjoyed
this short Christmas Tale,

It seems to bring joy
and hope without fail!

Here's Season's greetings
to folks far and near,

And wishes to all
for a Happy New Year!

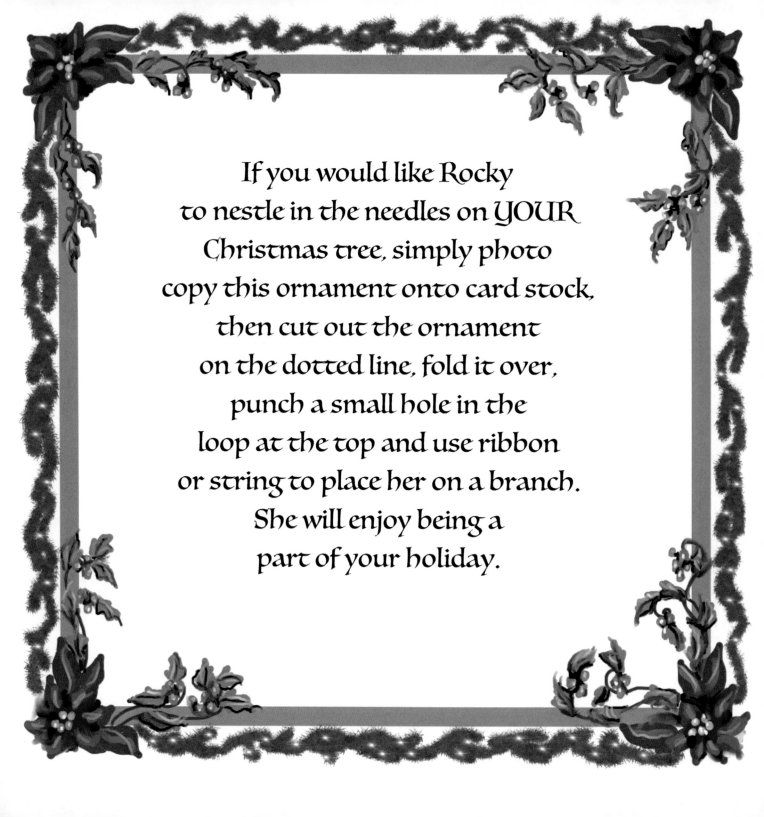

If you would like Rocky
to nestle in the needles on YOUR
Christmas tree, simply photo
copy this ornament onto card stock,
then cut out the ornament
on the dotted line, fold it over,
punch a small hole in the
loop at the top and use ribbon
or string to place her on a branch.
She will enjoy being a
part of your holiday.

A heart-warming tale based
on a true story, *Rocky the Christmas
Owl,* is sure to become a family
Christmas favorite. In the year 2020,
a tiny Saw-Whet owl was discovered
bundled into a very special Christmas tree.
This story recounts the tiny owl's adventure
in a way that charms and delights,
and the colorful illustrations bring the story
to life. A tale of a small miracle and of much
needed hope during a challenging year,
Rocky the Christmas Owl, is the perfect
addition to every Christmas story collection.

ABOUT THE AUTHOR

Bobbie Gilbert Kogok is a children's book author and illustrator.
Bobbie enjoys using art to bring a story to life and especially enjoys a story,
like *Rocky the Christmas Owl,* which brings hope and joy to the readers.
This is the fourth book Bobbie has written and illustrated, and she has had the
privilege of illustrating six books for other authors.

You can see her books and other art work on her website, www.bkpenandpaint.com or
on Facebook at BK Pen and Paint. Bobbie and her husband live just outside of
Washington, DC in Maryland.

Made in the USA
Monee, IL
29 October 2021